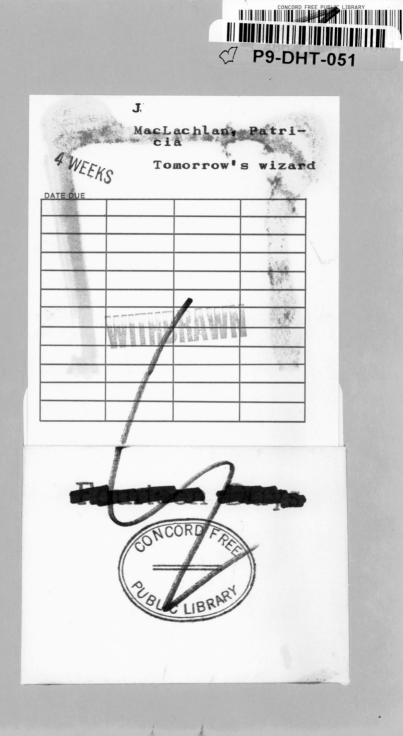

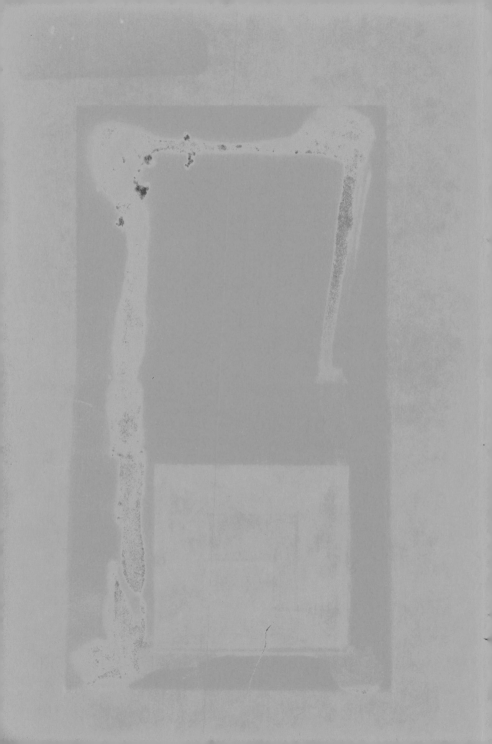

TOMORROW'S
WIZARD

TOMORROW'S WIZARD

Patricia MacLachlan

Illustrations by Kathy Jacobi

Harper & Row, Publishers

J.

Library of Congress Cataloging in Publication Data
MacLachlan, Patricia.
    Tomorrow's wizard.

    Summary: A wizard, his unorthodox apprentice, and
a wise horse make five important wishes come true in
ways that surprise the wishers.
    [1. Magic—Fiction   I. Jacobi, Kathy, ill.   II. Ti-
tle.
PZ7.M2225To 1982   [Fic]   81-47733
ISBN   0-06-024073-3   AACR2
ISBN   0-06-024074-1 (lib. bdg.)

This is for Bob—with love.

CONTENTS

TOMORROW'S
WIZARD

here is a wizard in the life of most everyone. Everyone, that is, who cares. There are those
who are mean through and through, those who
are jealous and those who spit at birds, and for
them a wizard would not help anyway. But for
the rest of the world, there is nothing so fine, so
magical, as feeling the touch of a wizard.

THE WIZARD

ong ago, but not so long as to embarrass anyone, Tomorrow's Wizard sat high in a tree looking at the world. The world, in fact, was quite wet. Rain had been falling for days. The wizard's long white beard was dripping and his feet made soggy noises in his green shoes when he wiggled his toes. He was bored, impatient and angry. Bored because he had been sitting for so long, impatient because he had heard no important wishes to answer in seven days and angry because High Wizard, who sat up on a cloud somewhere idly drinking honey tea in a large tin tankard, had sent him an apprentice.

Murdoch, the apprentice wizard, had a round face and was quite pale. In the rain, he looked like a boiled onion. And he was maddeningly cheerful. Tomorrow much preferred misery to cheer.

"Lovely rain," called Murdoch. He had settled in a damp bed of moss. "Warm and gentle."

Tomorrow groaned. He wished for an earthquake or a bolt of lightning.

"Have you heard any important wishes?" he asked gruffly. "Or curses?"

"Only for an end to the weather," answered Murdoch cheerfully.

"That was my wish!" grumped Tomorrow. He sneezed.

"Are you getting a cold?" asked Murdoch. "Perhaps you should wrap your beard about you."

"Wizards do not get colds," Tomorrow pointed out.

"I forgot," said Murdoch, sighing. "I keep forgetting about wizards. I spend so much time

among humans listening for important wishes."

"*Too* much time," complained Tomorrow. "There's only a fine line between wizards and humans. If you are not careful you'll forget about becoming a wizard."

Murdoch looked off into the mist.

"You may be right," he said thoughtfully.

"Wishes, wishes," prompted Tomorrow crossly.

Murdoch took a small paper from his pocket and read.

"Let's see. Farmer Mirth's wife wished for

a turnip, large enough for her stew. That's a wish we could answer. Such a nice family." He sighed again. "Happy, laughing children."

"Only a turnip?" complained Tomorrow. "That's small potatoes for me. *You* send her a turnip."

In his zeal, Murdoch sent Mistress Mirth a turnip that filled her empty horse stall. She would be using it, weather permitting, for months to come.

The rain fell on, and the fog drew around like soft curtains.

"Listen!" Tomorrow sat up. "I hear the hoofbeats of a horse. He sounds lame." He waved his arms mysteriously, making himself and Murdoch invisible.

In a moment, a horse did appear. It had thrown a shoe and was lame with a burden of vegetable sacks and a fat squire on its back. As Tomorrow had expected, the horse stumbled in front of the tree.

"Curses!" shouted the Squire, getting off to have a look at the lame foot.

"Curses is what we're here for," called Murdoch. "Curses and wishes."

"Who's that?" demanded the Squire, whirling around.

"Can't you ever hush up?" Tomorrow scolded Murdoch. He made himself visible. "Do you wish a new horse?" he asked, sighing. "One that is not lame?"

"Of course I do, you silly-looking wet old goat!" retorted the Squire.

"Rude," announced Murdoch.

"Who said *that*?" shouted the Squire, getting red about the face.

For once, Tomorrow was glad that Murdoch had spoken his mind. The Squire had been rude, and as a punishment the wizard exchanged the Squire's horse for a stubborn, foul-smelling jackass. And the Squire rode off on the donkey cursing louder than ever.

Once Tomorrow made Murdoch visible again, there was a long peaceful silence. Then Murdoch spoiled it by asking, "Where did you send the lame horse?"

High Wizard leaned over his tankard from

on high and spoke to Tomorrow. "You could tell him you don't know," he suggested.

"Wizards don't know everything," grumped Tomorrow, longing for peace.

High Wizard clattered his tin tankard warningly and Tomorrow jumped up. "I'm sorry, I'm sorry," he yelped. "Did you hear that?" he asked Murdoch. "You'd better beware!"

"Hear what?" asked Murdoch.

Tomorrow peered closely at Murdoch. The clattering of the tin tankard was a warning to all wizards. Even an apprentice such as Murdoch should be hearing it by now.

"You heard nothing?" asked Tomorrow suspiciously.

"Nothing but the wind and rain," said Murdoch cheerfully.

This made Tomorrow thoughtful. What sort of apprentice was this Murdoch? What sort indeed?

Murdoch's wishing brought the horse back. The horse was hungry, and it pawed the earth and nibbled on sweet leaves. It was friendly,

nuzzling Murdoch gratefully and nosing the
beard of Tomorrow, who was pleased in spite
of his temper. Besides, it was nice to have someone other than Murdoch to talk to.

"Why are you named Tomorrow's Wizard?"
asked the horse. He had a high, pleasantly nasal
voice, much like a viola. Or a tenor.

"Because I am not Today's Wizard," he re-
plied.

"Is there such a person?" asked Murdoch.

"I suspect so," said the wizard. "If I am

Tomorrow there must be a Today. I know there is a Yesterday. He lives over in the bayberry glen. He's very old and tends to ramble," he added.

"I don't understand," said the horse.

"Neither do I," admitted Murdoch.

"No one does," said Tomorrow. "Even I don't at the moment, my mind is such a jumble of unimportant wishes and curses."

"Never mind," said the horse kindly. "It's probably one of those things that everyone passes his life trying to understand, but that doesn't really matter one whit. Like beauty, happiness, or how long to boil porridge."

"Why, that's very philosophical," praised Murdoch. "I thought horses were not terribly bright."

"Some aren't," said the horse, not insulted. "But most are wiser than you think. I am very good at working figures in my head, and I can write decent verse. Sometimes I whistle."

"You do?" Murdoch was amazed.

"Hush," ordered Tomorrow. "You two are making so much noise with your jabbering that

I can't hear any important wishes or curses."

"If it's a wish you want, I've always wished I had a kind master and a warm barn," said the horse. "And a family of my own. Is that important enough? I even wished for that when I was born."

"Born?" said Murdoch, enviously. "You were born?"

"Of course. Weren't you?"

"Oh no," said Murdoch sadly. "Wizards and apprentice wizards aren't born. They just come about, like the sunset or a snowfall." Murdoch looked at the wizard. "Oh, how I would love to be born. Just once. Soft blankets, smiling family, brothers and sisters. I think being born must be heavenly."

"Stop!" hissed Tomorrow. "You are not to speak of heavenly matters. Wizards concern themselves with earthly things."

"I thought being born was fairly earthly," commented the horse. "However"—he leaned over to whisper to Murdoch—"babies cry when they're born. So it can't be all that wonderful."

"Eh? What's that?" asked Tomorrow, straining both to listen for important wishes and to hear what the horse and Murdoch were saying.

"He said babies cry when they're born," Murdoch said so loudly that the wizard jumped. "I thought you were supposed to be listening for important wishes."

Tomorrow was insulted and he began to sputter.

"I vow not to speak for a week!" he threatened. He folded his arms angrily, getting them firmly entangled in his beard.

"A whole week!" exclaimed the horse, impressed. "That's two feedings of grain and hay each day. Let's see, seven times two is fourteen. Fourteen feedings! A very long time."

"Never mind," urged Murdoch, ignoring Tomorrow. "Tell me more about babies being born. And crying."

Tomorrow's face puffed up with the effort of not speaking. Finally, he could stand it no longer.

"All babies don't cry!" he yelled.

"You said you weren't speaking for a whole week," chided Murdoch.

Furious, Tomorrow waved his arms in the air.

"Very well, then. A week! A week has just passed!"

High Wizard leaned over his cloud again and rattled the tin tankard warningly.

"Again!" exclaimed the wizard, watching Murdoch's blank face. Again Murdoch had not heard the rattle of the tankard.

"Oh," moaned the horse. "I'm starving."

"My poor stomach," wailed Murdoch.

"A whole week without food," said Tomorrow smugly.

The horse and Murdoch ran off to find food, so it was a long while before they spoke of being born and babies crying. In fact, Tomorrow was to regret making a week pass in an instant. For one thing, the minute they were gone he was strangely lonely. For another, he would find that a week's worth of wishes had piled up like dishes in a housemaid's washtub.

THE FIRST IMPORTANT WISH

Rozelle stomped her small feet up and down. She threw her gowns across the room. She howled.

The townspeople looked up from their suppers and smiled.

"It's only Rozelle," they said. They had learned that they could time their meals by the wails of Rozelle, for every day, strong winds or silent, she had at least three fits of temper. The sounds of her howling wafted down the hills, past every cottage. Each girl child was warned, "Mind you, you'll turn into a Rozelle if you're not well behaved." Every boy child was cautioned that he'd have a Rozelle for a wife if he weren't industrious and fair-minded. All parents said silent thanks that Rozelle was not theirs.

"A firm hand is all she needs," they agreed.

But Rozelle was not to know a firm hand. She had been born to her parents late in their lives. Rozelle's mother, a drab woman given to sick headaches, had never wished for anything but a sweetly singing bird. One that she could listen to when she wished and by covering its cage make it silent. But instead, she had a baby. The child, soft and pink like a flower bud, was named Rozelle. She bloomed into a fair rose of a girl, but like a rose garden left untended, she soon grew wild. And the thorns grew faster than the flower. Rozelle's too-gentle father, like many fathers, was so astounded by the blessing of a child that he saw only her beauty and forgave the rest. But the villagers did not. They soon grew weary of Rozelle's tempers and left her to herself.

"There'd be no trouble with the giant if Rozelle were set upon him," they joked. They joked, but they were fearful, for the giant was the only other cloud in a peaceful land. All lived in great dread of his distant trompings and rumblings. No one now alive had ever seen him, but there were many tales. One said that he had hair as black as thunderclouds and huge ears. Another said that he had great powers, and blamed him for a sick animal or a spoiled supper. Once, it was told, the giant had come down from his mountaintop in a fury and crushed a cottage flat beneath his great feet.

By the time Rozelle was a young woman, then, her weary father was twice worried. Like the villagers, he feared the giant. But he was also wise enough to know that his greater fear was that Rozelle would live with him for all of his days.

"Perhaps, with the aid of prayers," he told his wife, "there is someone in the land who will marry Rozelle. I will begin searching. Oh, how I wish for a husband for her!"

His wife put a hand to her brow. And she took her headache to bed, leaving her spouse with the task.

At the big tree, Tomorrow was out of sorts. A week of wishes had caught up with him. Murdoch and the horse, seven days of food heavy in their bellies, were complaining of aching stomachs.

"But at least the weather has cleared," chirped Murdoch.

"Let's hear this week's complaints, wishes and curses," Tomorrow ordered. He was combing crickets from his beard. In rainy weather they were apt to snuggle there, and he was horrified to find that one had chewed out a large chunk of white hair.

"Very well." Murdoch began counting wishes on his fingers. "Three clogged flues, two carts stuck in the mire, one flooded root cellar . . ."

"Unimportant, unimportant." Tomorrow waved them aside.

"Moldy grain at Miller Few's," Murdoch went

on, "a bushel of rotting apples at the Squire's"
(the horse snorted at the mention of his former
master), "a husband for someone named Rozelle
and thirty-three complaints about the giant."

"Stop!" called Tomorrow. "A husband for
who?"

"For whom," corrected Murdoch pleasantly.
"For Rozelle. But what about the giant? That
seems a more important wish."

"Or bigger," joked the horse, snickering.

"Forget the giant," said Tomorrow. "He's a harmless fellow, quite gentle."

"But the villagers don't know that," Murdoch protested. "Couldn't you let them know?"

"I have sent them many signs," said the wizard impatiently. "But they have been ignored."

"People rarely believe anything unless they see it for themselves," commented the horse.

"True," agreed Murdoch. He looked admiringly at his friend. "You know, sometimes it's hard for me to believe you're a horse."

"I'm a horse all right," said the horse, turning to nuzzle at his sore hay belly.

"Enough chatter," warned Tomorrow. "I'm thinking." He cupped his chin in his hands, an elbow on each knee. "A husband for Rozelle seems an impossible wish. Impossible! She is cranky, ill-tempered." He did a hopping dance and clapped his hands gleefully. "And because it is impossible, I will do it!" He skipped down the path, his green slippers flashing, making the barest of prints in the earth. He went straight to Rozelle's house and, making himself invisible, perched on a windowsill.

Inside, Rozelle's father was in a frenzy. What would Rozelle say? How would she react to his decision to find her a suitor?

"A husband for this peppy lass?!" she shrieked. Outside, Tomorrow covered his invisible ears with invisible hands. "Is there a man spirited enough for me?"

"Rozelle," her father cautioned. "A husband will be expecting kindness and gentleness in a wife."

"Tush!" shouted Rozelle. "A bit of fire never hurt anyone."

Her father sighed. " 'Tis a warmer fire by glowing coals than leaping flame," he said, wondering where he had ever heard that.

And so the word went out to all suitors. Tomorrow changed himself into a sultry wind that brushed the cheek of every lad and whispered the charms of Rozelle into each listening ear.

But that evening, Tomorrow returned to the oak tree in a thunderous mood.

"I sent a prince," he complained to the horse

and Murdoch. "But Rozelle's perfume was too much for him. Not to mention Rozelle! Then I sent a count, but she laughed at him." Tomorrow removed his slippers and blew on his tired feet. "There were old and young suitors, blacksmiths and beggars. There was even one small boy who brought Rozelle a nosegay of chickory blooms. She tossed them in the fire!"

"Perhaps you ought to turn your thoughts to the giant if Rozelle is so impossible," said Murdoch. "There are more rumblings, you know."

"Hang the giant!" yelled Tomorrow, making Murdoch and the horse laugh. "His only trouble is loneliness."

"Loneliness?" asked Murdoch softly. "I wonder . . ." The horse looked up, and in that moment the wind stilled, the animals paused in their foraging, the earth seemed to take a breath.

"Ah," murmured the wizard, looking at Murdoch. He nodded. "Tomorrow then. First thing."

The wizard waved his hands and dinner was before them: grain and molasses for the horse, and for Murdoch the tiny wild artichokes he loved. They ate well and slept soundly.

Morning brought a sun the color of bittersweet. But Rozelle was in a foul temper. She kicked the kitchen stools, stamped loudly on the wooden floors and hissed the house cat behind the hearth broom. Her father despaired and her mother retired with her morning tea and headache to the silence of her room.

Suddenly, there was a knock at the door. And when Rozelle opened it, there stood a man dressed in white and scarlet. He wore a hat with a tall white plume. Behind him was a splendid horse, the color of cream, with a jeweled bridle and saddle. The horse arched his neck and pawed the ground impatiently.

"Milady," said the man, "I've come to pay my respects." He bowed and his plumed hat brushed the floor.

But Rozelle's eyes were on the horse. It snorted, looked at her, and—could it be? It

smiled. Only slightly, but the horse *smiled*!

Rozelle smiled, too, and the cat came out from behind the broom. This horse was much finer than the prince, much fairer than the count.

"A ride upon my horse?" asked the man.

Rozelle nodded and brushed past the man. She jumped on the horse and galloped off, leaving the man at her doorstep. He smiled slightly.

Rozelle and the horse raced across the fields, leaping fences and bounding brooks. Faster and faster they galloped, across earthen paths and through the woods, until Rozelle finally cried, "Stop!" her curls popping across her face.

Before them was a lake the deepest blue color of a calm sky. And behind them stood a small forest of pine. Rozelle dismounted and walked to the edge of the water.

"Where is this place?" she cried. "Why have I not seen this before? Where are we?" She turned, but the horse had vanished. She was alone and lost.

She sat on a large rock near the water.

"Beg pardon," said a big voice near the tree-tops.

Rozelle jumped up.

"No need to be afraid," said the voice. "I'm just not used to anyone sitting on my shoe."

"I'm *not* afraid," insisted Rozelle bravely. She looked down and saw that the smooth gray that she had thought was a rock was indeed a shoe, with laces as thick as rope. She looked up into eyes the blue color of the lake.

"Why, you're the giant," she said boldly.

He leaned down and picked Rozelle up.

"Unhand me!" shouted Rozelle, wiggling and squirming within the giant's great grasp.

"Ah," said the giant, smiling. "You are Rozelle."

Rozelle pushed and struggled while the giant waited patiently.

Finally tired, she stared up into the giant's blue eyes.

"You know my name?" she said.

"I know your *voice*," said the giant. "Your

temper is more giant than I am." He looked
closely at Rozelle. "But your beauty is greater."
He laughed, and his laughter moved the grasses
of the meadow below and sent gentle ripples
across the lake.

To Rozelle's surprise, her face reddened. And
peering closer at the giant, she saw that one
of the tales she'd heard was not true. The giant
was handsome. Very handsome.

"Do you know," she accused him, "that you
frighten all the villagers with your rumblings?"

"Do you know that you do, too?" said the giant softly.

"*I?*" exclaimed Rozelle angrily. "*I* frighten them?" And she began to kick and squirm and shriek again in such a manner that the giant finally put her in his shirt pocket and closed the flap, smiling to himself. There was a long while of wails and muffled noises, but in time the noises stopped and the giant opened his pocket.

"My name is Ethan. And I know the villagers fear me," he said sadly. "I once trod on a cottage by mistake. I meant no harm at all. I was only looking for someone to talk to." There was a pause. "I am so lonely," he said.

In the darkness of Ethan's pocket, Rozelle's heart quickened. Loneliness? She peeked out of his pocket and looked up at the giant's large chin.

"But you don't have to be lonely, you know," she said. "You could have let the villagers know that you meant no harm. Although," she added thoughtfully, "it is sometimes hard to let people know what you really want."

"Ah," said the giant, peering down into his pocket. "I see you know about loneliness, too."

They talked of many things. And after a while, Ethan showed Rozelle the path home.

"Take me there," demanded Rozelle.

Ethan shook his head.

"You will find your way," he said firmly. And she walked down the long path, turning to wave more than once as Ethan stood with the last rays of the sun at his shoulder.

Days passed. And Rozelle's parents lived in peace. Even her mother came to sit by the evening fire. The villagers no longer timed their meals by the tempers of Rozelle. Two of them missed lunch entirely. And they all puzzled at the quietude of their suppers.

Each morning Rozelle awoke and ran to meet Ethan. He picked her up, laughing, and took her to where he lived. The chimney of his house touched the clouds. The curtains and rugs were dyed the colors of wild flowers.

"And it is a giant mess!" exclaimed Rozelle when she saw the monstrous dust balls under the tables. Together, happily, they cleaned. And when they ate, Rozelle sat on Ethan's huge carved table near his plate, small beside the flame of a burning candle.

Ethan had a giant dog named Wendelin, meaning wanderer. Some days Rozelle rode the back of Wendelin as they roamed the hills. Other days she sat, dreaming, beneath Ethan's great sunflowers and watched him as he worked. The days were peaceful and shared. And whenever Rozelle had a fit of temper, there was always Ethan's shirt pocket, safe and warm.

In the village, Rozelle's parents no longer spoke of a suitor, so content were they with their newfound quiet. But one day, late in summer, the wizard's wind whispers reached the ears of Ethan. The whispers still spoke of the desire of Rozelle's father to find her a husband.

Ethan heard. He listened carefully. And then, for only the second time in his life, he left his mountaintop.

Rozelle was in the garden when the great shadow fell across the valley. There were frightened screams and shouts from the villagers as

they saw the huge looming shape of the giant. They ran in all directions, calling, warning. All but Rozelle, who stood quietly surprised.

"Ethan!" she called to him. "Stop. Please stop where you are! You will step on the crops or on a cottage. You will hurt someone. Why are you here?"

Ethan stopped, bent down and picked Rozelle up in his hand, just as he had the first day they met.

"I," he said, "have come for courting."

"And I," said Rozelle, smiling, "I had almost stopped hoping."

It was a summer's eve when Rozelle married Ethan. The villagers called Rozelle a heroine who had sacrificed herself so that the village could live in peace. But Tomorrow, Murdoch, the horse and Rozelle's father, who had heard the gentleness of her voice, knew it was not heroism. It was love.

"You were beautiful," said Murdoch to the horse. "But it was your smile that did it."

30

"I have never had such a fine bridle and saddle," said the horse wistfully. "But you were quite splendid yourself in your white plumed hat."

"Hush," said the wizard, smiling at the two of them. "There are more wishes to come."

THREE-D

Miller Few was a demon. Not a demon with magical powers, but a rascal and a wretch. As a child, he had pinched the tips of cats' tails and squeezed their middles until they growled. He had soon been called Three-D for Dreadful Dastardly Demon. He had married a whiny, complaining woman named Mona who was as homely as a mushroom gone by. They had no children, but lived with a scruffy cat named Clifford, who had one eye and a nasty leer, which he turned on beggars and lovely maidens alike.

Three-D was the only miller in town, and he cheated all equally—rich and poor. He and his wife, Mona, had nasty natures. And they had no friends. It was most unfortunate for Murdoch that it was Three-D who saved his life.

If Murdoch had been a full-fledged and total wizard, he could have saved himself. But since he was still an apprentice and most often behaved like a human, he found himself hanging helplessly from a tree one day by only one bootlace.

"Help," he called feebly.

Tomorrow and the horse had gone off for a ride.

Murdoch was visited by three birds, a red squirrel and a family of possums, who hung next to him and stared curiously into his eyes.

When Three-D came along and cut him down from the tree, Murdoch was grateful. Three-D took Murdoch home for a cup of tea, and Murdoch saw their plight. They were out of sugar, the tea was bitter and, Mona told him, they had no friends.

"Perhaps I can grant you one small wish for saving me," he said.

Mona and Three-D fought for an hour over what wish they might be granted while Murdoch drank bad tea. Clifford stalked about, knocking dishes off the shelves and upending the flour. He stared evilly at Murdoch and batted at him from time to time.

Finally, Mona and Three-D told Murdoch that they wished a child. A sweet child.

"A sweet child," explained Three-D, "could work in the mill."

"A sweet child could put away the dishes and do the washing," said Mona.

At that point, Clifford bit Murdoch on the finger, so Murdoch decided to teach them all a lesson.

"I'll exchange you a sweet child for your cat," he said, for that much was in his power.

"This wretched cat!" exclaimed Mona. "Of course. Send us a sweet child."

And that is what Murdoch did.

Her name was Primrose. She had perfect

teeth like slipper shells, and red-gold hair that lay in tiny curls upon her forehead. She wore dresses of mauve silk with sashes and lace stockings. And no matter how hard she worked, she was never dirty. She dusted, washed and cooked better than Mona could have ever hoped to wash and cook. She helped Three-D in the mill, stepping primly among the sacks of grain so as not to soil her clothes. She was honest and courteous. And quite dreadfully sweet.

"No, Father dear," she would say in her correct small voice, "you owe the Squire more money. Don't you agree?"

"Mother, you should have added more meats to the pie. And there is a nasty speck of soot on your cheek."

After some months, Mona and Three-D found that they had many friends—because of Primrose. The friends brought them gifts and shared their suppers on many an evening. Life had changed.

They never fought or threw dishes at each other anymore, for it made Primrose cry delicate tears. They never used sour language to each other, for Primrose frowned, wrinkling her smooth, pink forehead.

It was all quite tiresome. Three-D longed to cheat and yell again. And Mona desperately missed her whining.

"I'm weary of all our new friends," Three-D whispered to Mona one evening. "They're all so proper, so refined."

Mona nodded. "If only we could go back to being wretched," she agreed. "Just the two of us. And that horrible cat, Clifford." A tear squeezed out of the corner of an eye and fell down her wrinkled cheek.

When Murdoch, Tomorrow and the horse heard this wish, they were overjoyed. Murdoch had taken Clifford back to the oak tree to live with them. And the cat had made them all miserable, especially the horse. He played with the horse's tail and sharpened his claws on his foreleg. He batted at Murdoch and pounced on the Wizard's slippers, tripping him up.

"This is your fault," the wizard accused Murdoch. "Why did you have to grant Three-D and Mona a wish? Couldn't you have said thank you and been on your way?"

Murdoch thought.

"Couldn't we just switch Primrose and Clifford?" he asked.

"Primrose here?" thundered the wizard. "I'd rather have Clifford! No, you'll have to find somewhere else for Primrose. It was *your* wish," he added irritably.

So Murdoch set off to find a new home for sweet Primrose. He knocked at many doors, but no one wanted a sweet child.

"How sweet?" asked the Squire.

"Very sweet," said Murdoch. And the Squire shook his head and slammed the door in Murdoch's face.

Murdoch walked the village up and down, but to no avail. Soon he reached the cottage of Three-D and Mona. He turned to see Clifford following him.

Primrose was in the garden picking daisies.

"A cat!" Primrose was delighted. And she bent down to stroke Clifford. But Clifford suddenly reached up to grab her hand, his claws leaving a long scratch of blood across her wrist.

Primrose's eyes grew round. Nothing like this had ever happened to her before. It was not proper. It was not sweet.

"You!" she shouted at Clifford. "Big, ugly, figgy cat!" She batted Clifford a whack across his head with her fistful of daisies. Then she chased him into the house and tossed the fire kindling over him.

Mona and Three-D came running.

"Clifford!" cried Mona when she saw him. Clifford had one claw stuck in Primrose's lace stocking. She ran, dragging him behind her. All of a sudden, Clifford let loose and flew across the room into the arms of Three-D. Clifford reached up and scratched Three-D across his nose.

"Clifford," crooned Three-D, overjoyed. "Welcome home."

Primrose threw a tinful of dried apricots on the floor and jumped up and down on them.

"Cat scratched! Cat scratched!" she shrieked.

"Why, Primrose," exclaimed Mona happily. "Your stockings are torn, your curls are scrambled, and your hands are filthy with fireplace soot. You look wonderful!"

Clifford jumped to the top of the cabinet and leered down at them.

"All is well," pronounced Three-D.

And from that time on, Primrose, Three-D, Mona and Clifford lived happily grousing, growling and grumbling ever after.

THE COMELY LADY
AND THE CLAY NOSE

Summer passed in its steady march to fall, and Tomorrow put on his red autumn suit and slippers. He made great show of changing from green to red, and the horse snorted in jest, for he was used to passing into each season with the same coat.

"Come now," Murdoch pointed out. "In the winter your coat grows thicker for warmth. The wizard should be able to change his clothing with some pomp."

So they celebrated the coming of autumn and the wizard's red outfit with Tomorrow parading

proudly, the horse nodding his approval and Murdoch applauding.

Suddenly, however, Murdoch stopped to stare, for coming through the woods was the most beautiful lady he had ever seen. She had long nut-brown hair and skin soft as smoke, and she wore a blue dress of silk. She was followed by a host of sighing young men. They swooned and fawned about the lady, and two fainted away directly in front of the oak tree,

their toes pointed to the sky.

"That's Geneva," explained Tomorrow. "She is so beautiful that the village boys lurk about, follow her wherever she goes and give her presents of flowers and ill-rhyming poems."

"She is comely," agreed Murdoch, who was feeling a bit faint himself.

"True," said the horse, "but why is she so sad?"

Geneva spoke then.

"Ah me," she said to herself, not noticing them there, "how I wish I could be loved for myself. 'Tis a trial to be loved only for my fair face."

"A wish! A wish!" whispered Murdoch loudly.

"There's your answer," Tomorrow said to the horse. "Geneva is *too* beautiful. So beautiful, in fact, that her true beauty is hidden." He sniffed. "Most of her admirers don't really understand about true beauty at all."

"You mean such as 'Beauty is only skin deep,' 'Beauty is in the eye of the beholder,' and 'Pretty is as pretty does?'" asked Murdoch.

"All of those," said Tomorrow, nodding.

"She is not just beautiful, though," observed the horse. "I can see her kindness. She may look like a peacock," he went on, "but I wager that she has the heart of a sparrow. Simple and pure."

"The heart of a sparrow," repeated Murdoch, delighted. "That's very poetic."

"Thank you," said the horse modestly. "I just now made it up." He tossed his mane. "Humans worry too much about their looks anyway. They're all pale creatures compared to horses. And their noses are too short."

Murdoch burst into laughter. But Tomorrow silenced him with an upraised hand.

"A nose, you say," he said thoughtfully. "Now that gives me an idea."

He ran behind the tree and returned with a green cloth bag. He opened the string top and peered in.

"Ah, marbles, moonstones and clay." He took out a round ball of cloud-colored clay. He warmed it and pushed it about in his hands. "It is true that Geneva can't help how beautiful she is," he crowed. "But *we* can help. A pinch here, a stroke there, and look!" He held the clay object over his head, quite proud of himself.

"What is it?" Murdoch walked slowly around the wizard, staring at the concoction. "Whatever it is, it's ugly."

"Yes, isn't it?" The wizard was delighted. "Three guesses now."

"A toadstool," said Murdoch, who hated guessing games.

"Wrong!" said the wizard.

"Well, then, a shoehorn," Murdoch grumped.

"Wrong again!" shrieked the wizard.

"A nose," guessed the horse.

"Correct, confound it," muttered Tomorrow, who hated losing guessing games.

"A nose!" exclaimed Murdoch. "I've never seen a nose like that. It's so long . . . and lumpy."

"Much too skinny and ignoble for a horse," agreed the horse.

"It's not for a horse." Tomorrow stamped his feet impatiently. "It's for Geneva."

"Geneva!" cried the horse and Murdoch together.

Tomorrow nodded his head up and down. "Now we'll see if Geneva really wishes to be loved for herself." And he ran off, stopping every once in a while to giggle.

He found Geneva peering at herself in the crystal pond. He tapped her on the shoulder and she whirled about, frightened.

"Who are you?" she cried to the strange creature in the red suit and slippers.

"I have come," said the wizard, "to answer your wish about being loved for yourself."

"You heard my wish?" Geneva was astonished.

"Is your wish sincere?" asked the wizard.

"I'm always sincere," protested Geneva.

"Always?" pressed the wizard.

Geneva paused and looked closely at Tomorrow. In his eyes she saw a certain power of observation.

"*Most* always," she admitted. "But I think I wish to be loved for myself."

"Whatever it might entail?" asked Tomorrow. The wizard knew the courage it would take for Geneva to agree to what he was about to ask.

Geneva took a deep breath and straightened her shoulders. "Yes," she said. "Whatever."

"Good," said the wizard briskly. "Then I can help you." And he produced the clay nose. "You must agree to wear this for a time."

Geneva looked. "A shoehorn? I must wear a shoehorn?"

"This is *not* a shoehorn," said Tomorrow irritably. "It is a nose."

"A nose!" gasped Geneva. Her hand flew up to touch her own comely nose. "It is a foul thing. A beak!"

The wizard smiled. "That it is. But if you are sincere, then you must agree to wear the nose."

"And if I don't wear it?" asked Geneva.

"Then," said Tomorrow softly, "you will never know."

Geneva thought.

"How will I know when I don't have to wear it anymore?"

"You will know," said the wizard, smiling mysteriously.

"Very well," said Geneva. "I will wear it."

The wizard was pleased. He fitted the ugly clay nose on her fair one.

"There."

Geneva looked at her reflection in the pond. The nose was long, monstrous, horrible. Geneva turned from side to side.

"It gives me some character," she observed.

Tomorrow was proud of Geneva, for the nose did make her more than a little unsightly.

The next morning Geneva adjusted her nose and walked outside. The dooryard was strewn with admiring gentlemen. Admiring, that is, until they looked closely.

"Zounds!" exclaimed the first gentleman. He was followed by "Egad!" "What ho?" "Horrors!" and "Bewitched!" The gentlemen fled in pairs and threes, east and west. And Geneva fled, too. She threw herself on the ground, weeping into her nose. She cried a long while as Tomorrow watched her from a treetop. But she did not remove her nose. And soon she gathered herself up and walked to town.

In town, the people gave her wide berth, dogs slunk away with their tails between their legs and children pointed. But Geneva walked on proudly.

For days thereafter Geneva was lonely. No one spoke to her or gave her the slightest nod. Instead, she spent hours walking in the woods,

discovering new wild flowers and watching the small animals that ran there. The mice, meadow voles and wild rabbits grew to know Geneva and her gentle nature, and she was comforted by their nearness. She seldom paused to look at her image in the pond.

One warm clear day, a wandering painter came upon Geneva feeding a family of sparrows. The birds sat on her shoulder and flew down to eat from her hand.

He stared at Geneva for a long time, watching her with the birds.

"How beautiful," he thought. And from his pack, he drew out a pad of paper. He sketched the scene, trying to capture Geneva's softness, her long careful hands, her smile as the fledglings chirped noisily for more. At last, he put his sketch aside and stepped from his hiding place.

The birds, alarmed, flew to a high branch. And Geneva, not having seen a human for days, fearfully raised her hand in front of her face to hide her nose.

But the painter called a greeting to her as if he hadn't seen.

"Good morning," she answered him. This man is kind, she thought. He does not speak of the nose.

"It is," he said. "I am Eric."

"I am Geneva," she said. "And these are my friends."

"Finer friends than many," said Eric, smiling.

They walked together in the woods, talking, and Eric looked back once to see a rabbit, a squirrel and the sparrows following. Unknown to them, Tomorrow watched down from the tree-tops, smiling through his long white beard. He scrambled down from the tree and ran to tell Murdoch and the horse.

"You mean they're friends?" asked Murdoch, delighted.

"More than friends, I fancy," said Tomorrow smugly.

And the wizard was right, for one day Eric asked Geneva to marry him.

"Marry you!" Geneva was aghast. "But my nose!" She raised her hand, amazed that she had not once thought about the horrible nose since their meeting. She was even more astounded to find that the long clay nose was no longer there.

Eric laughed. "What nose?"

"The long nose I had to wear," explained Geneva, puzzled. "Why, I was ugly."

"No," said Eric, taking her hands. "To me you were never ugly, from the first day I saw you until now. See, I painted you that day in the woods." And he showed her his drawing of her, surrounded by the sparrows. There was no clay nose.

They married in the woods with the animals about. Tomorrow wove a garland of flowers that he wound about them all: Murdoch, the horse, Eric and Geneva. And for a wedding gift, he gave them a statue to remind them all about true beauty.

It was a sparrow: small, perfect and made of cloud-colored clay.

THE PERFECT FIDDLE

here once was a fiddlemaker of good nature and great size. His name was Bliss, for he had been a happy child and his mother and father happy before him.

Bliss had a garden of foxglove, a warm wooden house and a wise wife named Maude. But even with all these, Bliss was not content.

"Alas," he cried to Maude one day. "I am miserable and morose, unhappy and generally sad."

"All of those?" said his wife sympathetically, smiling a bit.

Bliss nodded.

"But your fiddles are lovely and sweet and mellow," soothed Maude.

"They are that," agreed Bliss. "But there is one thing they are not."

"And what is that?" asked Maude.

"They are not perfect," said Bliss.

"Perfect!" exclaimed Maude. "And what *is* perfect?"

Bliss looked up at the sky and smiled at the sun.

"The sun is perfect," he said. "Such a bright golden color. Maybe that is the secret." And he eagerly set to work, finishing the fiddle at hand and gilding it to a shine like the sun, while Maude went out to sigh over the weeds in the garden of foxglove.

The next day, Bliss took the gilded fiddle to the fiddle master.

"It's a wonderful fiddle," said the fiddle master, smacking his lips with joy. "It speaks clearly. It's lovely. And it's mellow."

"Is it perfect?" asked Bliss.

"No," said the fiddle master. "It is not perfect."

Bliss went home, moaning to poor Maude. "Oh, I am miserable and morose, unhappy and generally sad," he complained.

Maude clucked her tongue over him and kissed him on his warm cheek. Then she made him a fine meal. For Maude knew that if there was not yet a perfect fiddle, a perfect meal there might be.

Bliss ate well. Then he and Maude slept, Maude dreaming of her dear husband, Bliss, and Bliss dreaming of a perfect fiddle.

At the oak tree, the wizard was weary from too much celebration. He had drunk a bit too much hum at Geneva's wedding, and his flowered hat tipped over one ear.

The horse was giving Murdoch a riding lesson.

"Squeeze a bit with your knees," he instructed pleasantly. And they walked around and around in slow circles that made the watching wizard even more dizzy.

"Halt!" he called finally.

"*Whoa* is the word," said the horse, stopping.

"There is only one wish today," said Murdoch, sliding from the horse's back. "It is Bliss, the fiddlemaker. He is miserable and morose, unhappy and generally sad."

"I know, I know," complained Tomorrow. "The same old wish he wishes. Over and over again."

"And what is that?" asked the horse.

"He wants," explained Murdoch, "to make a perfect fiddle."

"Is there such a thing?" questioned the horse. "Is there a perfect *anything*?"

"I am weary of this question!" said Tomorrow loudly. "Doesn't Bliss know that everyone, until he learns better, wishes for perfection?"

"What's wrong with perfection?" asked Murdoch. "It is my wish. It is being born."

"It is my wish, too," said the horse. "But it is a kind master and a warm barn."

"If it is anything at all," muttered Tomorrow, "it is peace and quiet from the two of you."

"Why can't you just give Bliss a perfect fiddle?" asked Murdoch.

"And be done with it," added the horse.

"That," said the wizard, growing impatient beyond his own imagination, "shows why I am a wizard, and why you are an apprentice, and why you are a horse! Now hush! And let Maude, who is most nearly perfect, settle the problem. There are some things that even wizards best leave be."

Morning bloomed through the shutters of Maude and Bliss's bedroom. And the birds began their morning chorus. Bliss awoke and ran to throw open the window. He heard the cascade of the thrushes, the sharp whistle of the cardinal and the sweet sad call of the mourning dove.

"Did you hear that?" he cried to Maude, who was knuckling the sleep from her eyes.

"The songs of the birds are perfect sounds. That must be the answer to the perfect fiddle!" And Bliss ran out, leaving Maude to smile at the ceiling.

"What a noodle," she said lovingly before she got up to cook the first meal of the day.

Maude fed her sheep and walked the lane

picking berries. Later, she bent her ear to Bliss's workroom door, hearing strange cries from within. But she paid them no mind, for she had heard stranger sounds from Bliss's workroom before.

That evening, Bliss brought out his latest fiddle to play for Maude.

"Listen, dear," said Bliss. And he began to play a series of trills and arpeggios. There were flappings and squeaks and chirps and tweets from his fiddle.

"What is that?" cried Maude.

"Birds," moaned Bliss unhappily. "Only birds."

And as Maude peered closer, she saw beaks pop out of his fiddle to pluck at the strings, and heard the flutters of their wings beating against the wood. And she saw the mess.

"Oh!" cried Bliss. "I am still miserable and morose, unhappy and generally sad. Poor me."

"Poor birds," murmured Maude as she cleaned up, comforted Bliss and helped him free the frantic birds.

And it was not to end. The very next day, after Bliss had heard the haunting moans and wailings of the wind, he ran out to capture the wind in a sock. And that night Maude watched him as he sadly played an imperfect fiddle, tapping his one white cold bare foot in the moonlight.

"That's not all!" said Murdoch, who was regaling Tomorrow with Bliss's escapades. "After hearing the sound of the waves against the shore, he actually flooded his fiddle with sea-water!"

"And played to the sound of drips," said the horse, "that did not keep time to the music. There's nothing more maddening," he added, because he was fairly musical.

"Stupidity!" shouted Tomorrow, out of temper completely. "There are serious problems about. I will not waste my energies on perfection. It is a bad state at best!" He thought a moment.

"What I will do," he said, smiling, "is visit

Maude. I've always rather fancied her. She is kind and has an honest smile."

Murdoch and the horse watched Tomorrow wander off through the woods.

"I never thought," said Murdoch, "that perfection was such a problem."

"That's because we're not burdened with it," said the horse matter-of-factly.

Tomorrow found Maude, rosy cheeked and like a flower herself, in the garden. She greeted him warmly, for they had been friends since she was but a girl and he an apprentice wizard himself.

"I thought you would be about soon," said Maude. And she sat on a tree stump and pushed her hair off her face.

Tomorrow sat on a pile of stones, and together they watched the beginnings of the sunset.

After a while, Tomorrow spoke.

"Don't you think, Maudie," he said softly, "that it is time to put the question to Bliss."

Maude sighed and lines ribbled her brow.

"I suppose I must," she said. She smiled and straightened suddenly. "Tonight I will make him turnip soup. It is his favorite."

"And then you will ask the question?" said Tomorrow.

"Yes," said Maude. "Then I will ask the question."

Silently, they watched the sun disappear. Then Tomorrow took his leave. Maude did not even see him go, so intent was she on thoughts of turnip soup. And the question.

That evening, Bliss was overcome when he smelled the turnip soup.

"Dear woman," he cried, throwing his arms about Maude. "You're a good wife. A fine wife."

Maude took a deep breath. It was the time.

"Would you say," she began, "that I am a perfect wife?"

"Perfect?" Bliss roared with laughter. "By heavens, no. What would any man wish with a perfect wife? If you were perfect, all our marriage woes would fall on *my* head."

Suddenly Bliss stopped, his soupspoon halfway to his mouth, as he realized what he had said. And then he knew.

"No one," he said slowly, "would want a perfect fiddle either. For the sour notes would be the fault of the fiddler."

"It would seem so," said wise and wonderful Maude, quietly sampling her soup.

Bliss smiled at Maude, and she smiled back.

And from that day on, Bliss made quite sure

never to make a perfect fiddle. Indeed, he worked hard at it, even smiling at the fiddle master's sour notes. And he was never again miserable and morose, unhappy or generally sad.

THE LAST IMPORTANT WISH

It was a windy day, and the sun would appear and disappear again behind the clouds in sudden waves of light and dark. Tomorrow was warm in his red autumn suit, and he was possessed by the mood that sometimes comes with changing seasons: the feeling that something was left undone. It was a mood not common to him, and he was uneasy.

The horse and Murdoch were frolicking in the lake of ice blue. They made loud happy noises and the wizard was jealous, which made him out of sorts.

"I wish it would hail and thunder," he said grumpily.

High Wizard rattled his tin tankard loudly, and Tomorrow sat up, calling to Murdoch. "Do you hear that? The warning again? We must get to work on wishes."

"Hear what?" asked Murdoch, laughing. "I might have heard something, but we were making so much noise." He dived under the water beside the horse, and they both came up near the bank, dripping water and shaking their heads in a shower of droplets.

"Did he or didn't he hear the High Wizard's warning?" mused Tomorrow. "What does this mean?" The questions ran through his head, making him more restless.

Murdoch and the horse lay down on the bank, hoping for some warm sun.

"I used to water at a swimming hole years ago," said the horse wistfully. "The Squire's children used to ride me there, three of them at once, and let me drink. Then I'd rest while they swung out over the water on a rope."

"A rope?" Murdoch propped his head on a hand and gazed at the horse.

The horse nodded.

"They would swing out, out, over the water, then drop into the deepest part." He frowned. "Sometimes it is hard to be a horse. I used to beat them at every footrace, though," he said, brightening.

"Races?" Murdoch called to Tomorrow sitting on a high branch of the tree. "We never run races. Could we do that?"

Tomorrow shook his head, strangely sad. "I'd win always," he said. "I have powers, you know."

Murdoch sighed. "That's right. I keep forgetting about wizards."

The tin tankard rattled again, making Tomorrow sit up straight and nearly fall off his branch. He peered through the leaves, but Murdoch was laughing with the horse. He stared at Murdoch for a long time. Then he swung through the branches of the tree, scrambling down limbs like a young monkey on his mother's arm.

He took Murdoch by the shoulders and turned him around.

"You hear nothing?" he asked urgently.

Murdoch cocked his head to one side.

"Maybe, maybe I heard something. Something very faint. I thought perhaps it was thunder." Then, seeing the sad look on the wizard's face, he reached out to touch him. "Why does that make you so sad?"

Tomorrow shook his head.

"Never you mind." He patted Murdoch on his arm, a sign of affection he had never before shown him. "Are there any important wishes or curses?" he asked hopefully.

Murdoch shook his head.

"No. The giant and Rozelle are happy, Three-D and his family are pleasantly discontent, Geneva and Eric have no wishes, and Bliss and Maude are imperfect. The Squire has his usual minor troubles. There are flooded root cellars, rat problems . . ." He stopped as the wizard waved his arm.

"Except," Murdoch said slowly.

"Except what?" asked Tomorrow.

"The horse. He talks of children, a family. He still longs for a kind master and a warm barn."

"But the three of us," said Tomorrow. "We've been like a family, haven't we?"

"Yes," said Murdoch kindly. "We have. Almost. But for swinging out over the water on a long rope, and footraces. And children."

There was a silence. Then Tomorrow sighed.

"Very well," he said, his face set so as not to loose the tears. "Do you wish to say good-bye to the horse?"

"No," said Murdoch softly. "I don't think I could do that."

"No," echoed Tomorrow with a slight smile. "I rather think you won't have to say good-bye."

He waved his arms before him. And the horse, standing serenely by the water, suddenly pricked up his ears. Before you could say "Tomorrow's Wizard" quickly, the horse was standing in a horse stall next to the largest turnip he'd ever seen. He was warm and groomed to a shine.

"A horse!" cried children's voices. "Our wish has been answered. Mama, Papa, come look. A beautiful horse for the farm!"

Farmer Mirth came running and called his wife to bring a bucket of oats.

"Ah, he's so handsome," she said when she saw the horse. "And he looks so wise." She put out a gentle hand to stroke his mane.

"You did that very well," said Murdoch back at the tree. He stood close to the wizard, their shoulders touching. "I shall miss him, though."

"Not for long," said Tomorrow briskly. "Patience."

High Wizard nodded and smiled, and sent down a sudden blanket of sun to cover the forest.

"Let's ride him!" shouted the eldest Mirth child. But as he climbed on, the horse wheeled and plunged. Everyone tried, but the horse allowed no one on his back.

"Such poor luck," moaned Farmer Mirth. "What good is a horse if he can't be ridden? The fields can't be plowed, and we'll have to walk the long road to town."

"Say it," urged Tomorrow out loud.

"Say what?" asked Murdoch, mystified.

Farmer Mirth's wife spoke then.

"Only, if only . . ." she began.

"Only if only what?" prompted Tomorrow loudly.

The tin tankard rattled and Murdoch looked up. And suddenly he knew. He knew, as surely as if it were written on a page before him, that he was about to be granted his own most important wish.

He turned to Tomorrow.

"I'll not forget you. Ever!" he said fervently.

"Oh yes you will," said Tomorrow with a sad smile. "But I won't forget you."

"If only someone could be sent to us who could ride the horse," finished Farmer Mirth's wife at last.

And as she spoke, there came a soft noise from the cottage. There, lying in a straw basket, wrapped in soft blankets, lay a baby. He was as pale as the moon, with a face just as round. He smiled, and his new family smiled back.

Never once did he cry.

In time, the baby grew into a strong, gentle and loving child. And to the amazement of all, by the time the child could walk he could also ride the horse. The fields were plowed and the farm prospered. Often, the boy rode the horse into the hills and played about an old oak tree. Sometimes he swung out on a long rope over the water while the horse rested.

Tomorrow, as invisible as a morning mist, could almost touch them both.

"They are happy," he told High Wizard. "But I miss them so."

High Wizard smiled and nodded.

"Yes. The line between wizards and humans is very fine indeed. Some choose to hear the warning rattle of the tankard and some heed

76

other voices. You did well. You knew the difference."

Tomorrow sighed. "Yes, but only . . ." He looked guiltily at High Wizard. "I know wizards are not supposed to wish important things themselves, but I wish there was one remembrance for them. One small glimmer from the past."

High Wizard saw Tomorrow's sadness. He shifted a bit on the cloud and his old shoulder began to ache. He looked down at his gnarled hands, rubbing his knuckles for comfort. And he made a decision.

"You know"—he turned to Tomorrow—"one day soon you will be High Wizard. I shall tell you a secret that will ease your loneliness."

High Wizard suddenly sat up straight and rattled his tin tankard. Then he pointed down to earth.

The boy, riding the horse, suddenly reined him in. He stopped and cocked his head as if listening to a faraway voice. The horse's ears rose forward, listening too.

Tomorrow stared earthward for a long while.

Then he smiled.

"You mean," he began, "that some hear the
High Wizard's rattle, some hear human voices,
and . . ."

"Yes," said High Wizard, smiling. "And some hear both.

"And now," said High Wizard, leaning back and closing his eyes, "can we listen for important wishes?"

"Yes," said Tomorrow. "We will listen."

And to this day they do.